THE THORN

VALLA SERIES NOVELLA - BOOK 3.5

ANNA REZES

WORDS
IMAGINED

ALSO BY ANNA REZES

Valla Series:

Unraveling Emily-book one
Descendant of Valla-book two
Guardian of Latovia-book three
Broken Alliance-book four

Pink f*cking Moscato

ISBN: 978-1-950657-13-1(paperback)

ISBN: 978-1-950657-14-8 (ebook)

This is a work of fiction. Names, characters, places, and incidents are either a product of the author's imagination or are used fictitiously. Any resemblance to actual persons, living or dead, events, or locales is entirely coincidental.

Cover design by German Creative

First Edition: 2019

Words Imagined

Hilliard, OH

www.annarezes.com

To those who are kind in the midst of their own suffering.

CHAPTER 1

HER HEART POUNDS SO FRANTICALLY that she's afraid the men will hear it. She knows they'll hear her thoughts before hearing her heartbeat. But if they hear her thoughts, they'll know she's worried about how loud her heart is pounding, and they'll probably laugh at such a stupid idea.

"Keep going, Morgan," Alec whispers behind her.

She didn't realize she had even stopped. She crawls forward, down the center of the dirty circular storm drain. She counts her blessings that it's mostly dry.

"We just need to get far enough away," Alec reassures.

No one appears to be following, but it's unlike the Olvasho to get their hands dirty. Morgan figures they're likely walking around above ground, waiting them out, but she is counting on them having no idea where this field irrigation storm drain ends. It curves underground and splits into two smaller tunnels. When they come to the fork, Morgan unlatches the grate and leads them left, which will take them to the woods at the edge of her parent's property. She knows because she and Alec used to get in trouble for playing in here when they were younger.

They got smarter about it and started taking the route that led them into the woods so they wouldn't get caught.

It all feels like a million years ago as Morgan crawls into the narrowing tunnel. It's only two feet high here, and she tries not to think about the soft things squishing between her splayed fingers as she crawls. She doesn't remember it being so disgusting or feeling so claustrophobic, but they were smaller back then.

"Only 50 more yards. We got this," Alec encourages, following closely.

She can't imagine how cramped he's feeling. She looks back, but can't see anything in the never-ending darkness. "Are you gonna get stuck?"

"Hope not," he says.

That's when they hear the scurrying paws. Alec grabs Morgan's ankle. "Stop."

"Do you think we can scare them away?"

"We have to be quiet. I wish I were in front of you right now."

"Give me your shoes," she says because her flip-flops won't do. She listens as he moves around in the sludge behind her. And then his tennis shoes poke her in the butt.

"Sorry."

She reaches back and slips her hands into them. "I'll try to nudge whatever it is away with the shoes on my hands."

She moves forward more slowly, swiping at the space in front of her, paying close attention to every sound and any sign of movement. They find a beacon of dim light shining ahead. With the faint light, Morgan picks up her pace. She reaches the grate, sticking her hand through to unlatch the closure, only to realize debris blocks the grate from opening. Morgan puts her shoulder into it, but it only budges an inch. She tries again and gets nowhere.

"Alec, sit back to back with me. I'm going to kick it open."

"Give me my shoes back and let me kick it. I'm gonna lay flat, and you climb over me."

She crawls over him, and he says, "Fletch, you stink."

"Seriously, you're joking around right now?"

"Trying to lighten the mood, so I don't focus on the Olvasho trying to kill us," he whispers before leaning back to back with Morgan. He kicks the grate, springing it free and making a loud noise as it clatters into the creek below.

"Shit!"

Morgan pushes him. "Go!"

He jumps out of the drain, landing a few feet below in the shallow stream. He turns to help Morgan, but she's already jumping into the water, landing more gracefully than he did.

They both look around the small tree-covered ravine. It's only April, so most of the trees are pretty bare, but the coast appears to be clear. Morgan isn't taking any chances. She grabs Alec's hand and runs along the stream away from the drain and away from the Olvasho chasing them.

"I'm never letting you talk me into leaving my phone behind ever again," Alec complains.

"Shh," she says, spinning on him. It was a bad day to wear flip-flops, but the weather was unseasonably warm.

She lets out a squeak as her foot slips. Alec reaches for her, but she's already falling. The back of her head collides with a stone, and everything goes dark.

CHAPTER 2

FIFTEEN YEARS AGO ~

"Alec, slow down!" Morgan yells, running after him through the field behind her parent's house. "You're too fast!"

Alec slows, letting Morgan catch up to him, "Mowgan, you just gotta wearn to be fast wike me."

"One day I'm gonna be faster than you," she tells him as she sprints past him in her muddy clothes.

"No, you won't. You'll nevah be as fast as me," he laughs as he runs ahead of her. "Your wegs awe too short."

"But they'll grow." She stops, looking down at her legs before laying on her back in the grass.

Noticing she stopped, Alec backtracks, standing with his hands on his hips. "What awe you doing?"

She lifts her muddy foot toward him, wiggling her bare toes. She took her shoes off earlier after they got wet and she forgot to put them back on. "Pull on my leg. It'll grow faster."

He grabs her ankle and begins pulling, but she slides across the grass.

"You gotta hold onto somefing," Alec says.

They move to the edge of the porch so Morgan can hold onto the steps while they try it again.

Julie, Morgan's mom, steps out onto the back porch of their country home, asking, "What are you two doing?"

As Alec continues to pull on her foot, Morgan yells, "Mom, Alec's helping me grow my legs!"

Julie says, "I think that's enough for today. If they grow too fast, they'll fall off."

Alec's eyes go wide and he lets go. Morgan jumps to her feet, and they climb onto the porch.

Looking them over, Julie says, "Morgan, what happened to your shoes?"

Morgan gives a guilty smile. "They got wet."

Julie takes a deep breath. "You guys went into the storm drains again, didn't you?"

Morgan and Alec look at each other, both covered in dirt, and Morgan has leaves tangled in her long brown hair.

With a sigh, Julie says, "Go rinse off in the lake and then I want you inside right away. Wait." She notices blood mixed with the mud stains on Alec's dark shirt. "Alec, honey, are you bleeding?"

"It's okay. Mowgan fixed it. She made me a bandage and got the bweeding to stop."

Julie steps forward, moving his hair off his forehead to inspect the cut.

Morgan chimes in, "I'm gonna be a nurse, momma. It was bleeding a lot, but I didn't even faint. I just covered it with mud and leaves until it stopped."

Morgan doesn't understand why her mom looks so worried, but then she realizes that her mom isn't a nurse like she is. "It's okay, momma. If you faint, I'll take care of you. I'm a junior nurse," she says proudly.

Julie swallows, saying, "Morgan, go rinse off in the lake. Alec, you come with me."

Morgan doesn't budge. "Alec shouldn't be in trouble. It wasn't his fault."

"No, he's not in trouble, but it's not a good idea to put mud in a cut."

"But it stopped the bleeding. I fixed it."

"It could be infected."

Morgan slaps her forehead. "I forgot to check if it was infected."

Her mom pushes Alec into the house while Morgan goes out to the lake.

CHAPTER 3

MORGAN COMES TO, hearing the familiar beeping of a monitor. She opens her eyes, looking straight up at the clear bag of fluids hanging from the IV pole. Why is she in the hospital? How did she get here? Then she remembers the Olvasho chasing them. She jerks up, throwing the blankets off and winces, squeezing her eyes closed as the room spins and her head throbs.

"Easy." The voice is right beside her, but she can't open her eyes until the pounding in her head slows. She feels a hand on her shoulder, and when the spinning stops, she looks to see Alec.

"Alec, what are we doing here?"

Jerrick enters the room. The massive man's muscles ripple through his shirt. Morgan thinks he looks like a younger, darker version of The Rock, and she instantly feels safe with the intimidating man, knowing he can protect them.

Jerrick says, "How are you feeling?"

Morgan takes in the space, realizing they aren't in a hospital at all, though the hospital equipment is very real. "I'm okay. Where are we?"

"Below Mark's Security office. His assistant, Chris, is a trained EMT. He took care of you until I could get here. You have a concussion. Head trauma is difficult to heal. I did my best for now, but I can't sense all the damage until the swelling goes down, and I can't use my gifts to decrease the swelling without risking more damage. If you start feeling dizzy or your headache worsens, let me know."

"Where is Mr. Burk?"

"Mark and Chris are upstairs combing through surveillance. It seems you were followed home from the mansion a few weeks ago. An Olvasho named Keith has been following you, waiting for the right moment to try to trap you."

"What about everyone else? My parents, my sister, Ben, Molly, Sam, Cindy?"

"They're okay," Jerrick says, "After you hit your head, Alec carried you to the neighbors where he called Emily, and I answered since she's handling other matters. I arranged for Mark to pick you up and bring you here until I could get here. Mark looked at the surveillance from your homes and the homes of your loved ones, and Keith hasn't visited anyone else."

"My house doesn't have surveillance," Alec says.

Jerrick explains, "As soon as you learned our secret, you joined the surveillance list. There are plenty of Olvasho who believe in killing people who know our secrets. Emily has claimed you as her people, which should make you untouchable. The moment Keith followed you, he declared himself an enemy. He waited to come after you until you were isolated without a way to call for help. If you stay hidden too long, Keith will get skittish and go into hiding. We need him to keep pursuing you so we can catch him. I'm sorry to rush you, but we have to leave."

Alec sets her clothes on the bed next to her. She hadn't

even realized she was wearing a hospital gown. "Did you wash these?"

"Yes, but we don't have time for you to shower. You've already been here too long," Jerrick says.

Morgan looks at the IV still in place. "I need a cotton ball or something."

Alec goes through drawers until he finds a Band-Aid. "Here," he says, handing it to her.

She takes the oxygen sensor off her finger and pulls out her IV. When the monitor beeps, Alec turns off the machine. "We'll step outside so you can get dressed," Alec says, but Morgan is already stepping into her pants.

"It's not a big deal. I still have my bra and underwear on," she says, fastening her pants.

She unties her gown, letting it fall before slipping into her shirt. She watches Alec struggle to give her privacy. He tries to keep his eyes on the floor, but eventually, he peaks up at her. Trying to hold in her grin, she slides into her flip-flops and announces, "Ready!"

Morgan and Alec follow Jerrick out of the underground bunker, up to Mark's office, where Mark and Chris are watching surveillance feed on multiple screens.

"Morgan," Mark says, getting out of his seat. "I'm glad you're okay."

He hugs her, and she replies, "Thanks for your help."

"I'm sorry we didn't notice him before he got to you. He did a good job of staying out of sight. He only slipped up a handful of times, but now that we know who we're looking for, our software knows his face and will alert us whenever he's spotted."

Jerrick clears his throat.

Mark gives Morgan another quick hug, saying, "You'll be safe with Jerrick."

"Thanks, Mr. Burk, for everything."

"Anytime. You know that."

They head out of the office and into the giant black SUV that sits right outside. Morgan and Alec climb into the back while Jerrick takes the driver's seat. The windows are so deeply tinted that the sun almost disappears.

"Is this car bulletproof?" Alec asks.

"Yes," Jerrick says.

"Where are you taking us?" Morgan questions.

"A safe house. Somewhere Keith isn't familiar with. It'll take us an hour to get there."

"How do you know he'll follow?"

Jerrick glances at Morgan in the rearview mirror. "Because he put a tracker on your phone."

"You have my phone?"

"Yes." Jerrick continues, "Keith is a coward, he won't attack unless he's sure he can win. He doesn't know I saw his face, or I'm sure he'd be more aggressive. I'm taking you to a safe house where I will pretend to leave you so I can lure him in. I'll take him off guard and catch the people helping him."

"So, we're bait?" Morgan says.

"Yes, but you'll be safe the whole time," Jerrick promises.

"Can we have our phones back?" Alec asks.

Jerrick's eyes stay on the road ahead. "When we get there, I'll take the trackers out and give them back to you."

Morgan rests her head on Alec's shoulder and touches the back of her skull, feeling matted hair over the sensitive skin.

Alec whispers, "You scared the shit out of me, you know. You hitting your head like that. You could've died. There was so much blood coming from the back of your head."

"That's because you didn't pack it full of mud and leaves."

Alec laughs and kisses the side of her head. "I'm not a junior nurse, like you," he laughs. "I'm glad you've learned a few things since then."

"Yeah, sorry, I could've killed you."

"You're probably the reason I'm dyslexic."

She nudges him with her elbow. "That's terrible to say."

"Relax," he soothes, "I'm kidding."

Morgan rolls her eyes. "Hilarious."

CHAPTER 4

SIX WEEKS AGO ~

Morgan sits in her car at the curb outside the salon. She flips down her visor to check her face and flips it back up. Shaking her head, she mumbles, "Get it together, Morgan. It's just Alec. Stop overthinking everything."

She rolls down her window, glad the weather is warming up. The March air teases of spring, and the sun warms her skin while she continues to overthink.

Since she broke up with Preston, she can't stop thinking about Alec. Actually, it was even before Preston. She and Alec have been friends since preschool, and she was fine pretending there wasn't more between them until her friends brought it up last summer. Her drunken confession that she loved him in the fall complicated things for sure. Especially because he thought his girlfriend was pregnant at the time. It led to the biggest fight Morgan and Alec had ever had. They had only recently begun patching up their friendship. She is afraid to be more than friends with him because he had let her down too many times in the past.

So, if she isn't interested in more, then why is she making sure her long brown hair is laying perfectly straight and that her light blue eyes pop against her dark mascara coated lashes? Why had she even put makeup on? She rarely wears any, and Ashley already had her wearing nail polish and tinted lip gloss. But how much of that was for her, and how much was for Alec?

As she's wiping off her lip gloss, the door to the salon opens. Alec walks out, spotting Morgan at the curb. He gives her his swoon-worthy smile complete with dimples and sparkling hazel eyes. His brown hair is cut in a short, trendy style. He'd always been attractive, and as he climbs into her passenger seat, she takes in his amazing scent, reminding herself that she can't trust him with her heart. Sure, she trusts him to keep his knowledge of the Olvasho a secret, but he'd always been a trustworthy friend, just a lousy love interest.

"Thanks for picking me up, Fletch."

She smiles as if he doesn't affect her the way he does. "What happened to your car?"

"I took it in for an oil change, and they found a leak in the transmission. It should be done in a few hours.

As Morgan pulls away from the curb, Alec asks, "Do you have any cash?"

She shakes her head, no.

"Can you take me to the ATM?"

"Sure, does the car place only take cash?"

"No, while I was getting my hair cut, the stylist next to mine went on her lunch break. The other girls were talking about her and how she's a single mom who's been eating Raman noodles every meal just so she can get gifts for her son's birthday. I wanted to take her some cash."

Morgan stays silent as another piece of her tries to fight her feelings. "You don't think they're taking advantage of you?"

"I mean, maybe they're pulling one over on me, but I doubt it, and I'll feel like a piece of shit for not helping when I have the means to do something."

"But I thought you were saving up to get your own place and for school and now your car."

He looks over at her, asking, "Do you think I'm making a mistake?"

Morgan swallows and shakes her head, "No, I wanna help, too."

"You don't have to do that."

"Neither do you."

They pull up to the ATM, both withdrawing money before taking the short trip back to the salon. Alec asks, "Will you take it in? I don't want her to know it came from me. I don't want her to think I'm interested in her.

"I don't even know who to give it to."

"Her name is Shelly."

"Umm, okay." Morgan runs in and drops off the money.

Once she's back in the car, Morgan says, "So where to?"

"My mom's birthday is next week. Would you be willing to go to the mall with me and help me find something for her?"

"Of course!" Morgan guides them toward the mall, asking, "Do you know what you want to get her?"

"I don't know, probably some sappy mom shit."

Morgan elbows him. "You have the best mom. You better be getting her a sweet, sentimental mom gift."

"I'm not good at shopping, but I feel like I need to get her something good this year."

Morgan's phone rings from her purse on the passenger side floor. "Will you get that?"

He pulls it out. "It's Ashley."

She holds out her hand for it, but instead of giving it to her, he answers, "Hey, Doll." There is a beat of silence, and then Alec says, "Shit, slow down. What?"

Alec puts the phone on speaker, but Ashley is already mid-rant. "—head exploded all over Emily. Lathe lost it! He dragged the shooter across the lawn with his mind and—"

"Ashley, what is going on?" Morgan asks.

"I think I'm in shock," she says.

"Did you say someone's head exploded?" Morgan really hopes she misheard.

"Evelyn's dead," she sobs, "and Lathe . . ." Her words die as sniffling takes over.

"Is anyone else hurt?"

"Lathe killed the shooter."

"Where are you now?"

"In Evelyn's room. Oh my God, I think I just found—Oh shit! What was that?" Ashley cuts away, and they hear footsteps followed by a howling wind and then static. "Oh my God! What's he doing?" Ashley fumbles with the phone before saying. "I gotta go."

Morgan sets the phone down and at the next intersection, turns away from the mall. Heart pounding, she pulls onto the highway that will lead them to Fort Wayne. "I need to see what's going on."

"Are you sure it's safe for us to be there?"

"No, but we have to do something."

"But I don't think it's safe to be there right now."

"Alec, I need to be there for my friends!"

"I know, but maybe just take a breath first. There is an exit up here. At least let me drive. You're shaking."

She looks at her trembling hands and flips on her blinker.

THEY NEVER MAKE it to the mall. Alec takes over driving, taking them to Morgan's apartment, where he tries to comfort her. When they finally get a call from Patrick, he explains the situation and informs them of Evelyn's funeral. He encourages Morgan to wait until the funeral to come.

Alec puts his arms around her and kisses her forehead, saying, "This is right. You should wait."

When Morgan drops Alec off at his car that evening, she wants to ask him to stay with her, but that's not something friends ask of each other no matter how frightened and anxious she feels.

Before she pulls away, Alec stops at her window, leaning in, he asks, "I know this has been a rough afternoon. Is there someone you want to call to stay with you or something? I'd stay but don't know that Preston would be too happy about that."

It takes her tired brain a minute to wonder why he's worried about Preston, and then she remembers Alec still doesn't know they broke up. "Thanks, Alec. I might spend the night at my parent's house."

He nods. "You'll let me know if you need something, right? Like tissues or a hug or to help you grow your legs longer."

Tears of sadness overflow the rim of her eyes even as she smiles at the memory. He always knows what to say to make her smile. Deep down, she doesn't know if it's because he really cares or if it's just his God-given charm. Lord knows he's charmed the pants right off dozens of women.

He had changed since Sadie and her fake pregnancy, but Morgan remains cautious, especially now. She busies herself with her seatbelt, so she doesn't do something stupid, like pull his face in the window and kiss him.

"Thank you, Alec. I'll let you know if I need you."

CHAPTER 5

MORGAN IS NUDGED AWAKE. "HEY," Alec says. "You shouldn't sleep yet."

From the front, Jerrick says, "You still have a concussion. I'll check you when we get to the house. It's not far now."

Morgan watches as Jerrick's finger taps against the steering wheel. It's almost hypnotic, and then she notices his jaw, tight and tense, grinding.

Alec can't see the signs of irritation since he's right behind the driver's seat, so he's oblivious to the tension when he asks, "So, what exactly is the plan?"

Jerrick's jaw releases and he sighs while his hands grip the steering wheel tight. He glances back. "It's better you don't know."

Alec makes a face, unhappy with that answer. Morgan senses the tension, so before Alec responds, she squares her shoulders, ignoring her headache, and says, "Jerrick, I'm sorry you have to deal with this. You probably feel like you're babysitting."

His grip on the steering wheel tightens, his knuckles

turning white as he inhales long and deep. He glances in the rearview mirror, his words barely more than a growl. "I've had my doubts about Keith. I know what people like him can do to people like you." His breathing is labored and his teeth grind.

Jerrick is usually warm and personable, but Morgan has only seen him when Emily and Patrick were present. Maybe his friendly personality is a front.

"I'll destroy him before it comes to that."

Alec and Morgan exchange a worried glance while Jerrick turns into a residential neighborhood. The streetlights flicker to life as the sky darkens. He pulls the giant SUV to the side of the road, and sighs. Soon, a man that looks like a smaller version of Jerrick taps on the passenger side door. The man is about the same height but without the muscular bulk.

Jerrick puts the car in park, saying, "You guys stay here." He gets out and rounds the SUV, speaking to the man on the sidewalk.

"Do you think that's his brother?" Alec asks.

He turns to Morgan, and she squints out the window, her vision getting blurry. She blinks a few times, trying to clear her view, but eventually has to shrug and close her eyes to keep her headache at bay.

"I think they're arguing," Alec narrates.

"I've never seen Jerrick so angry," Morgan says, referring to earlier.

"He looks pissed right now. This SUV must be soundproof. I can't hear what they're saying."

"Siblings argue," she grits with her eyes squeezed closed. "Alec, my head hurts so much. I feel fuzzy, and I'm suddenly so tired."

"He said the house isn't far, but maybe we should have Jerrick look at you now."

"Far from what?" she mumbles.

"The house."

"What house?" she asks, unsure what he's saying.

"Morgan, do you know where you are?"

Where is she? She knows it's a simple question, but her mind is so fuzzy. Then she remembers—her memories coming back sporadically. Her eyes don't open as she responds, "On the bus, but can we slow down, I'm getting dizzy."

Alec leans over to roll down his window, calling, "Hey, something's wrong with her!"

"Shh," she shushes, her head objecting to the sound.

CHAPTER 6

FIVE WEEKS AGO ~

ALEC MAKES a second attempt to get something for his mom. The mall is busy this evening but not so busy that he misses Morgan's boyfriend walking toward him. Preston makes eye contact, and Alec inwardly groans, reminding himself to be kind. This is just another reason he fucking hates shopping.

"Hey, Alec, how're you doing, man?" Preston says it like they're best friends, but Alec hardly knows the guy, and he doesn't really want to know him. The guy is a tool. He doesn't understand what Morgan sees in him. Even Alec can see Preston isn't right for her.

"Hey," Alec says, "Just picking up something for my mom's birthday."

"Get her a flower bouquet. Mom's love that stuff," Preston says.

"I need to go all out this year. It's her fortieth."

"Sure, sure, so how's Morgan doing?"

His question throws Alec. Had she told him about Evelyn

passing? She was probably vague about it, but why would Preston be asking him. "What do you mean?"

"Just wondering how she's doing after the break-up. I didn't know if she heard I was already in a new relationship. I was kind of worried about her, but you know, it's not like we ended on bad terms."

Alec feels blindsided. When had this happened? "When did you break up?"

"Oh, have you not talked to her? We split a few weeks ago. She made it sound like you guys were close."

Alec lets out a breath, realizing he doesn't have to be nice to this asshole anymore. He steps forward, standing over Preston, AKA bag of dicks. "Did you break up with her?"

Preston steps away, looking unsure about the sudden change in Alec. "I, eh, it was a mutual decision."

Alec grinned, "She dumped your pompous ass, didn't she?"

"I should've known I couldn't keep her. She didn't care about the fancy stuff," Preston says, trying to laugh it off, but Alec knows he's intimidating him. Pussy.

"No shit," Alec says.

Alec doesn't care to stay and listen. He walks past Preston and into the jewelry store he can't really afford. He wants to buy his mom the prettiest damn necklace he can find within his measly budget. Thank God his mom didn't care for all that fancy stuff, either.

He finds a simple necklace that has his birthstone intertwined in the cursive letters that spell out *mama*. He's not good at buying gifts, but this has to be better than the macaroni necklace he made when he was six. And she wore that stupid necklace until it fell apart. To this day, its remains still hang on the hook next to her real jewelry.

He pays for the necklace and leaves the mall, dodging Preston on his way out. Damn, does the guy just hang around the mall? Then he sees the girl with Preston and laughs. She looks like a Morgan wannabe, but she is definitely the knockoff because he is on his way to find the real one now.

ALEC SECOND-GUESSES himself as he stands outside her apartment. She is going to Indiana in the morning for Evelyn's funeral. Alec can't go because of work, and the only reason he'd be going is for Morgan. He paces up and down the sidewalk. He already texted her that he's dropping by, so if he doesn't go in, she will wonder what happened to him.

"Fuck it," he says before walking up to her apartment. He knocks as he opens the door.

Morgan looks up from her spot on the couch when he walks in. "Hey, Alec. I wasn't expecting you so soon. I'm still studying." She tilts her head. "Why are you smiling at me like that?

He closes the door and leans against it, his smile growing as he focuses on her.

"What?" she says with a grin.

His smile slowly melts as he stares at her, his nerves making him second guess his next move, but it's Morgan for fuck's sake. He pushes off from the door to join her in the living room. He sits down on the coffee table in front of her—his eye contact so intense, it has Morgan blushing.

"Alec?" she questions.

He leans forward, his elbows on his knees. "I ran into Preston today?"

He watches her panic. "Preston—"

He presses a finger against her lips to quiet her. "Did you lie so I wouldn't make a move on you?"

Morgan nods, his finger still on her lips. He pulls it away, saying, "That's fair, but will you let me know when I can?"

She stares at him, her face unreadable.

Maybe he's coming on too strong, but he doesn't know how to do this. Morgan isn't just a chick he wants to bang. She is everything.

Instead of speaking, she reaches out, laying her hand on his arm. She taps her finger against it. Two taps, pause, and one more tap. It's the secret code they invented in first grade. They used it as a sign of solidarity whenever one of them got in trouble, but Morgan never got in trouble. It was always him, yet she never gave up. The taps said, "We're in this together. You and me."

At least that's what they used to mean.

"I love you, too," he confesses, not sure exactly when it changed or if that's what it's always meant.

Her gasp is almost silent. "Alec, I can't—"

"It's okay." Before he does something crazy, like kiss her, he stands and walks to the door.

"Have a safe trip tomorrow, Fletch. Are you still riding with Mr. Burk?"

"That's the plan. We leave after my last class tomorrow afternoon."

"How are you feeling about going?"

"I need to be there. I need to support them any way I can. I may not have known Evelyn well, but my heart breaks for Lathe and the others. It's so sad."

CHAPTER 7

Jᴇʀʀɪᴄᴋ ʜᴀɴᴅs ɪɴᴛᴇʀʟᴀᴄᴇ on top of his head. He lets them fall to his sides as Alec calls for help, and he and his brother walk to the vehicle. Jerrick opens Morgan's door, touching her, using his gift to sense the slight internal bleeding inside her skull.

"This is my brother Dominic," Jerrick says, stepping back. "He'll help her."

Jerrick rounds the SUV and settles into the driver's seat while Dominic slides in on the other side of Morgan.

Closing the door, Dominic says, "Wow, it stinks in here."

Alec explains, "It's her hair, we didn't have time to wash it. Is she going to be okay?"

Dominic places a hand on her head and seems to concentrate before saying, "Probably."

"Probably? What does that mean? What's wrong with her?"

"It's harder to concentrate with your mouth running," Dominic says.

Alec shuts up, and they drive in silence for several

moments before the house comes into view. Jerrick drives past it, unable to bring himself to stop. He hates his brother for doing this to him. He debates going to a hotel, but then their plan won't work. Jerrick has no doubt that Dominic did this to him on purpose. He rounds the block and slows this time, but still keeps driving.

Dammit. He is going to murder Dom.

He glances in the rearview mirror as he does another lap around the block. Alec looks confused, wondering what's going on as he recognizes the same row of houses. Jerrick turns his attention to Dominic, healing Morgan.

"How's it going?" Jerrick asks.

"It'd be better if we weren't in a moving vehicle," Dominic says. "If you could stop this time, that'd help."

When the house comes around again, Jerrick pulls into the driveway. The house looks beautiful, well cared for, thanks to his brothers, no doubt.

He sits there while Dominic tells Alec to carry Morgan inside, and soon the vehicle is empty aside from him and the ghosts of his past.

He can't do this.

He can't be here.

CHAPTER 8

FIVE WEEKS AGO ~

EVELYN'S FUNERAL was to take place at the Fort Wayne estate. Morgan rides out with Mark. As they pull into the gated drive, Morgan is surprised by the number of cars parked on the side of the long paved driveway. She didn't expect so many.

"Are we late?" Mark asks.

"No, it doesn't start until three."

"Who are all these people?" Mark asks as people dressed in black suits and gowns walk up toward the main house.

"Oh, my," Morgan says, "I feel underdressed."

"Maybe this is how Olvasho funerals are." Mark shrugs.

"I bet Lathe will hate this," she says.

"No one was there for her while she was alive, but they all show up now. Yeah, I think he's justified in his anger."

Mark parks, and they begin their journey to the mansion door. "There must be hundreds of people here," Morgan says as they walk into the circular foyer. "Will we even be able to find Emily?"

Jerrick suddenly appears in front of them. Morgan doesn't understand how someone so big could come out of nowhere, but she is relieved to see him. "Jerrick," she says, "how's everyone doing?"

Jerrick shakes Mark's hand, saying hello before answering Morgan's question. "Currently, they are upstairs, hiding from the masses." He turns toward the stairs and says, "This way."

Jerrick leads Mark and Morgan through the mansion toward the entrance to the balcony. He holds the door open for them before disappearing.

As they walk out onto the balcony, Ashley and Lathe are huddled close in an intimate embrace, and Emily and Patrick are hugging while Deja appears to be on guard duty. The seven-year-old gives dirty looks to anyone who dares to glance up at the balcony.

Patrick spots the newcomers and whispers into Emily's ear, causing her to break their embrace. She turns to hug Morgan before greeting her dad. Mark motions with his head toward the door, he and Emily disappear.

Morgan wraps an arm around Patrick, asking, "How are you doing?"

"None of us took her death well."

She notes, "Jerrick seems to be holding it together."

Patrick gives a dry laugh. "He can't even stand to be in here with the rest of us. He's someone you want next to you in a disaster because he keeps his cool and functions logically, but after the trauma, he isolates himself. I suspect so he can fall apart in private. I'm glad he was there the day Evelyn died, but her death may bring up some of his past demons."

"He has past demons?"

"He spent a year of his life being blackmailed by Sky. We all have our demons. Jerrick, more than most."

"He seems so level-headed."

"Remember, Morgan, the Olvasho are master manipulators. You can't take anything at face value."

Morgan swallows.

CHAPTER 9

Dᴏᴍɪɴɪᴄ ʟᴇᴀᴅꜱ Alec into the house and throws a blanket over the couch before directing Alec to lay her there. Alec sits at her feet while Dominic continues to do whatever it is he's doing.

"Why is it taking so long?"

"Head injuries are tricky. Jerrick is better at this. Once he comes in, he can take over."

"What the hell is he doing?" Alec stands, walking to the front window where he sees the black SUV. The windows are too dark to see if Jerrick is still in there, but he had to be.

"Give him time. He'll come around," Dominic says.

"He didn't want to come here, but you made him. You switched plans on him, didn't you?"

"Plans just change sometimes."

"Where are we?"

"You're safe. That's all that matters right now."

Alec points at Morgan. "She is not safe. She needs Jerrick!"

"I'm keeping her safe until Jerrick comes to take over."

"Fuck that! I'm gonna go get the bastard!"

CHAPTER 10

FOUR WEEKS AGO ~

MORGAN KNOCKS at the door as she walks into Alec and Cindy's house for their standing Sunday dinner. "Hey!"

"In the kitchen," Cindy calls, "You're the first one here."

"I thought Molly usually helps you," Morgan says, coming into the kitchen.

"She does, but she and Ben had some legal paperwork they needed to finish, so they're running late, and Alec is still at work.

"On a Sunday?"

"Yeah. They're behind on a contract, so it's all hands on deck until the construction is finished. He's been working crazy hours."

"I thought he was just avoiding me," Morgan says, not realizing she's saying it aloud. She holds out the little gift box to Cindy.

Cindy grins. "What's this?"

"Happy belated birthday. Sorry I missed it."

"It was just the other day. It's still my birthday week. You didn't miss it."

Cindy opens the rectangular box and reads the paper within. Her eyes jerk to Morgan's. "An all-inclusive spa day." She shakes her head. "I can't accept this! This is way too much."

"You're going. You deserve it, and besides, Patrick paid for most of it. Trust me, he can afford it." Morgan smirks.

Cindy gives her a look. "That cousin of yours sure is generous."

"It's not as nice as your necklace," Morgan notes, looking over the delicate chain with Alec's birthstone and letters that scrawl out *mama*.

Cindy's face fills with warmth, and her hand wraps around the letters with a wistful sigh. "Oh, my boy. He spoils me. I finally feel like I got him back, Morgan. I know you played a part in that. You being sweet, and Ashley laying the Smack-Down. I love that girl. I heard her yelling at him one day on the phone, telling him to get his head out of his butt. She seems to speak his language while you are this calm presence that makes him want to be a better man. Someone who deserves you."

Morgan gnaws her inner cheek and looks at the floor, unsure how to respond.

"I guess that bitch, Sadie, played a part in Alec changing, too. Although, I'd really rather not give her any of the credit." Cindy continues, "Now, exactly how long ago did you and Preston break up?"

Morgan looks surprised.

"Oh please, it's obvious," Cindy says. "At first, I thought you avoided bringing him up in front of Alec, but even when Alec isn't around, you don't talk about him."

"I wasn't trying to lie," Morgan says.

"I know that. Just like you know my son is crazy about you.

I don't blame you for being cautious, but he seems like he's got himself sorted. He hasn't been on a date since Sadie."

Morgan's heart pounds. "I don't know if I'm ready."

The front door opens with a knock and then paw's scrape against the hard floor. Cindy quickly says, "Take your time. Make sure you're ready because I think he's all in."

Max, the giant Newfoundland, bounds around the corner into the kitchen and spins around Cindy and Morgan. Molly enters next, followed by Ben.

THEY ALL SIT around the kitchen table, and Alec joins them, fresh out of the shower. Morgan gets a whiff of his body wash as he takes the seat next to her.

"Hey, Fletch," he says, piling food on his plate. "How was the funeral?"

She gives him a look. "Sad. Ashley comes home tomorrow. I'm pretty sure Lathe is coming with her while she finishes her last three weeks of school."

Cindy breaks in, "I feel so bad for him, losing his mom so suddenly. And Lathe being one of the first at the scene . . . how awful."

The outside world believed that Evelyn and another woman were in a head-on car collision, and both women died at the scene.

"So, Ashley and Lathe sure got serious quickly," Cindy comments, changing the subject from death.

"I guess they met last fall," Morgan says.

"We should invite them for dinner next Sunday."

Molly chokes.

Morgan offers to invite them while Molly coughs and sputters.

Once she catches her breath, she says, "I know his mom died and all, but does he have to come here? He's scary."

Ben gives her a warning look, while Cindy says, "Molly, hun, what's so scary about him?"

"Everything. His scars. The way he looks at everyone like he wants to kill them."

"What?" Morgan laughs.

"He's scary," she continues, "He just is. I don't know. I can't, like, explain it."

"I get what you're saying, but he makes Ashley happy, and I trust her judgment," Alec says.

"Maybe he won't seem so scary in a different setting."

"Doubt it," she says under her breath.

Cindy ignores it and asks, "So how's school going for you, Morgan?"

"Almost done! I'm only taking one class this summer, and I can't wait to have some time off."

CHAPTER 11

"Morgan, wake up."

She hears Alec calling to her, but her eyes are so heavy. When they finally open, Alec is looking down at her. She is content for a moment before all her thoughts and questions catch up to her. Questions like: Where is she? How did she get here? Why is she so tired?

Alec looks relieved to see her, and before she can ask, he says. "You hit your head. You still have a slight concussion. What's the last thing you remember?"

"I remember running by the stream, and my foot slipped because I wore these stupid flip-flops." She looks down at her feet on the couch. But who's couch? "Where are we?"

"I'm not sure," Alec mumbles, glancing into the other room where a hushed argument is taking place.

"Who is that?"

"Jerrick and his brother. I don't know what's happening, but Jerrick is acting weird."

He fills her in on everything she missed, finishing with, "When Jerrick finally came into the house, he healed your head in like five seconds and walked away. His brother went after him, and they've been arguing since."

"How did I not see someone following me from the mansion? I've tried to be so careful."

"It's not your fault. They all missed it. We're supposed to be protected, and these people have abilities we don't."

"Still, I should've seen it."

"I forgot you were Miss Perfection." Alec gives her a warm grin before something crashes in the other room, and the voices get loud.

Jerrick shouts, "Then so be it!" He storms by the living room and out the front door.

Morgan grabs Alec's hand, asking, "Does he still have our phones?"

Alec shakes his head. "That dude is scary. I wasn't about to ask for them when he's acting like that."

"Emily always said he was the calm one."

"Then I'd hate to see what the rest of them are like."

Dominic walks into the living room. "How are you feeling?" he asks Morgan.

"Confused," she answers, thinking he looks like a less bulky version of Jerrick, from his dark skin, stunning blue eyes, and his height. He was intimidating but not like Jerrick.

"My name is Dominic," he says, "I'm glad to see you awake. You both need to take showers. I can't take that smell. And change out of those clothes. There are clean clothes in the room down the hall, last door on the left. Help yourself to anything that might fit. But please shower!" His phone rings and he answers, saying, "Hey, honey." He covers the speaker, adding, "Bathroom is on the right." He walks out of the room, speaking into the phone. "You know how he is. He'll come around."

Morgan and Alec look at one another. Morgan says, "This is weird. I want to call Emily."

"Apparently, Jerrick has her phone too, so . . ."

"Maybe we can call Patrick then."

"Let's go shower, and then I'll see if I can use Dominic's phone."

"Okay. Is it bad that I can't smell myself?"

Alec smiles. "Well, you hit your head pretty hard, maybe it knocked a few marbles loose."

"You should've just patched me up with some mud and leaves and called it a day," she says.

"You said the same thing earlier."

"Weird. What else did I say earlier?"

"You told me how excited you were to shower naked with me."

Morgan laughs as she sits up, saying, "Are you sure you didn't knock a few marbles loose?"

Alec smiles. "I'm staying in there with you in case you relapse and fall or something."

Morgan stands slowly, and Alec leans in, helping her to her feet. They take the hall back, finding all the doors closed. They go to the last on the left and find a fully furnished bedroom with a king-sized bed. Sure enough, the closets and dressers are full of men and women's clothing.

"Who lives here?" she asks.

Alec pulls out an extra-large t-shirt from a drawer, wondering, "Could it be a safe house?"

"I don't know. Patrick said Jerrick has demons. Maybe it's the home of someone he killed. That might explain why he's so upset."

"Wait, is he a killer?" Alec whispers.

She shrugs. "Sky was blackmailing him, but I don't know the details. We shouldn't talk about this here, anyway."

They both find clothes and leave the bedroom.

Morgan says, "I wonder which one of these is the bathroom."

"He said it was on the right."

The first door they try is a laundry room. "At least we can wash our clothes. I know you said you washed them earlier, but my hair got everything gross again."

"I don't like wearing someone else's stuff."

"Especially when we don't know who it belongs to," Morgan adds, opening the door to the bathroom.

Alec sits on the closed toilet and reads the home and garden's magazine from two years ago while Morgan showers. He hands Morgan a towel, and she wraps herself in it before sliding open the shower curtain. While she towel-dries her hair, Alec gets in the shower.

She slips into the pajama pants and top she found in the other room. She gathers their dirty clothes, saying, "Alec, I'm going to see if there is laundry detergent so I can wash our clothes."

"Okay. I'll be quick."

She carries the things to the laundry room, happy to find soap. She starts the load and then heads back to the bathroom, but on her way, notices the door across from the bathroom is cracked. It's the only room she hasn't seen. She slowly nudges the door open and freezes in the doorway as the light from the hall pours into the dark space.

Morgan flips on the light and takes in the blue and green bedroom. There are dinosaurs painted on the walls and a dinosaur toddler bed with a T-Rex comforter.

A little desk set with markers and colored paper stood by the door, and scribbled drawings hang on the walls. This room wouldn't be in a safe house. A little kid lived here. Curious, she walks into the room, spotting a decorative board, painted like a giant ruler hanging on the wall. Along the top in scrolling letters, is the name, *Jackson*.

Morgan's fingers brush over the last height marked, dated two and a half years ago. She gets a sick feeling. This isn't something you leave behind.

Then from right behind her, she hears Jerrick's voice, breathy and questioning. "Victoria?"

Startled, she spins, instantly terrified as his face morphs into something that spreads fear to every nerve in her body. His hand clamps around her bicep, and he yanks her out of the room, slamming the door closed and shouting in her face, "Who told you, you could wear this?"

Before she can answer, he demands, "Take it off!"

Tears come to her eyes, and the bathroom door flies open, Alec bursting through dripping wet with only a towel around his hips.

Dominic appears at the end of the hall, saying, "I told her she could."

Jerrick drops her arm to prowl toward his brother while Alec goes to comfort Morgan.

CHAPTER 12

NEARLY THREE YEARS AGO ~

JERRICK CRACKS the kitchen window before pouring coffee into his mug. He looks over his shoulder to where Victoria is struggling to get Jackson to settle in his booster seat. Breakfast is not usually this much of a struggle with the little guy, but he didn't sleep well last night.

A woman's screams come from outside, high-pitched, grating, and terrible. It sends a chill through Jerrick, and he turns toward Victoria, who pauses what she's doing to stare at him with anxious eyes.

"I'll check it out," he says, setting down the coffee while reaching out with his mind to scope the surrounding area.

As he heads out of the kitchen, moving toward the front door, he hears more shrill screams and grabs his cell phone from the hall before exiting the house.

Stepping outside, his anxiety increases when he sees his mother's car parked out front. Then he finds her, kneeling by the flowerbed at the side of the house. He walks across the porch and looks over the railing.

His blood runs cold.

"My baby," his mother whimpers as she holds her hands out, not sure where to touch the body lying in front of her.

Stacy's eyes have always been bluer than Jerrick's, but right now, they stare up at him, milky and unseeing. Even in death, she is beautiful, but her rich dark skin is pale and ashy.

Her clothes are ripped, and her skin is gashed and bruised, making it obvious his baby sister fought for her life. But someone was stronger than her, and he instantly knows who to blame. Sky's men had just come through town. He saw the way they looked at her, but he never imagined . . . This.

Something snaps inside him. Enough is enough. Jerrick is a peaceful man, but he can no longer do nothing. He wants vengeance.

CHAPTER 13

JERRICK THROWS Dominic against the wall. Morgan grabs Alec's hand, tugging him into the laundry room.

Alec pulls the door closed behind them just as a loud crash echoes from the hall. "What the Hell?"

Morgan wipes her tears. There's no time to cry. She's glad she was snooping around earlier because it's always good to know an escape route. She walks through the narrow room, past the washer and dryer to the door opposite the one they came in, saying, "This leads to the kitchen."

She cracks the door, peeking into the kitchen. A cell phone lies on the table. She tries to get a glimpse of the guys, but they're still in the hall. "Stay here," she says before darting out to snatch the phone. She hurries back into the laundry room and closes the door.

"Who are you calling?"

"Patrick," she says, typing in his number.

"You have his number memorized."

"I memorized a lot of things when my life started getting crazy." She hits send, putting the phone to her ear.

"Dominic?" Patrick answers.

"It's Morgan. Long story. Jerrick is acting scary. I think he might beat his brother to death."

"Did Dom provoke him?"

"I don't think so. Jerrick lost it when he saw me. He called me Victoria. Who's Victoria?"

"Morgan, where is he now?" Patrick asks.

"In the other room. We're hiding."

"Put me on speaker and go out there."

Alec is shaking his head, no. But Morgan is her own person, so she goes to the door. Alec grabs her arm.

She turns to him. "Alec, he's going to kill his brother. We have to do something."

"Then let me do it," he says, "You might trigger him again."

"Fine," she huffs, handing it over.

He takes the phone out into the hall, but the brothers moved into the living room. Alec is careful to avoid broken glass in his bare feet.

Entering the room, he puts the phone on speaker and says, "Okay, Patrick."

"Jerrick," Patrick says through the phone. "This isn't what Victoria would want. She wouldn't want you to hurt your brother. Don't let your grief turn you into something you're not. Don't let Sky win."

Jerrick turns to face Alec, who is still only in a towel. Jerrick stalks toward him and Morgan steps between them, causing Jerrick to hesitate.

Morgan says, "I'll change, Jerrick. I didn't know."

She gets a glimpse of his emotions before he turns away and storms out of the house.

Dominic picks himself off the floor, wipes at his bloody face, and runs out after Jerrick.

Morgan takes the phone from Alec. "Patrick, how did you know that would work?"

"There is only one thing that makes Jerrick lose his mind."

"Victoria," Morgan says. And even though she's certain she already knows, she asks, "Who was she?"

"His wife."

She walks back down the hall, opening the dinosaur bedroom that Jerrick dragged her out of. "And they had a son?"

"Yeah."

She looks at the ruler on the wall with a new understanding. "What happened to them?"

"Sky happened," Patrick says.

She covers her mouth as tears overflow.

CHAPTER 14

TWO AND A HALF YEARS AGO ~

JERRICK IS glad more people don't have his "gift." Controlling the liquid in a person's body is a gift unique to him. It is dangerous, which is why he never told anyone aside from close family what he can do. He had honed his skill the best he could without actually practicing on another human being until now.

He steps over the two men lying face down on the floor. One suffered a massive heart attack and the other an embolism. Neither died of natural causes. Jerrick killed them. His first murders. He never wanted to become a killer. He had always been a peaceful man, believing in structure and order, but how can he stand by when he has the potential to stop the men that killed his sister and the dozens before her. But they aren't enough. He will kill his way to the evil man that leads them, making them nearly untouchable. He won't stop until he cuts off the head of the snake, so to speak.

He watched Sky destroy their people for too long. It has to end. Suddenly the doors to Sky's private chambers are thrown open, and a baby-faced blond teenager comes through. Everyone knows Patrick, Sky's protégé. He's supposed to be without conscious, but as Jerrick takes him in, Patrick stares at the scene before him. Jerrick senses his pulse. Both men are Isa descendants, which makes it a little more difficult for Jerrick to take control.

Patrick's eyes flick up, looking at Jerrick with hope. A hope that speaks of the end of Sky. Their eyes catch, and an understanding takes place. Jerrick releases his hold on the boy, and Patrick steps out of the way, holding the door for Jerrick. He silently invites him into Sky's guarded private quarters, aiding in the murder of his mentor. Maybe their relationship isn't what people thought.

Jerrick enters the grossly decadent room. Velvet curtains, silk cushions, and satin sheets on the unmade bed. Sky has his back turned, sitting at the edge of the bed, looking like a normal man, but he is no normal man. At roughly two centuries old, Sky looks to be in his early forties with platinum hair that hangs past his shoulders. His skin is pale, and he has a slender build making him appear harmless.

Jerrick reaches out with his mind and takes control over the blood in Sky's body before he even realizes he has company. Jerrick's hands lift into the air to maintain control as Sky mentally fights back. Jerrick's gifts continue to pour out, holding the evil man's blood, trying to slow it, but he can barely maintain control. His hands tremble, and his taut arms shake. The sheen of sweat spreads over his dark skin, and droplets form on his forehead. Jerrick feels sweat gather and drip down his thick muscled back. He grinds his teeth, bearing down as he holds Sky suspended in the middle of the room.

"Her name was Stacy!" Jerrick shouts, walking forward while he forces Sky's blood to stand still.

CHAPTER 15

Patrick is still on speakerphone. "Sky's men raped and murdered Jerrick's sister. He killed all the men involved with his sister's death, and he went after Sky, but Sky just wouldn't die. In fact, Sky was so impressed by his gifts that he made him an offer, and when Jerrick refused, Sky kidnapped his wife and son. He held them hostage for almost a year before Jerrick could no longer comply. Sky had Jerrick's family murdered and threw Jerrick in prison. I don't think he's been back to his house since."

"That's why they were fighting," Alec says. "Jerrick didn't want to come here. He was fighting with Dominic about something. There was some kind of last-minute change of plans. Jerrick drove past this house three times before pulling in. It's the home he lived in with his family."

"How did you guys end up with Jerrick?"

"I tried to call Emily. He has her phone. Said she was dealing with Olvasho issues or something."

Patrick laughs, "Or something. Such a diplomat. Emily

received some rather disturbing news and has become a bit unpredictable. Did you call Lathe?"

Alec says, "I tried to call Ashley, but she didn't answer, and I don't have Lathe's number. Morgan is house-sitting for her parents. We were out on a boat. Morgan said we should leave our phone in case the boat flips."

"You flip a boat every year," Morgan justifies.

"I guess Keith followed Morgan home from the mansion a couple of weeks ago," Alec continues. "He waited until we had no way to contact anyone before him and two others showed themselves. They tried to manipulate us on the boat, but their reach was weak, and we managed to get off the boat and run through the field. They had us cornered, but we lost them in the irrigation storm drains. Then Morgan hit her head. I got us to the neighbors where I called Emily, but Jerrick answered and had Mark pick us up. They went back and looked at the footage, realized it was Keith. Jerrick brought us here and said he's going to use us as bait to weed out Keith."

"Sounds like you've got things under control," Patrick says.

Morgan is sitting on the floor, holding a stuffed dinosaur. She looks up at Alec, saying, "I'm wearing his dead wife's clothes and snooping in his son's room. And he doesn't even want to be here. I have to change." She stands, carefully placing the stuffed animal on his bed before she walks out the door.

CHAPTER 16

EIGHT DAYS AGO ~

Morgan enters the house without knocking. Cindy's car isn't out front, which means it's only Alec. She finds him in the living room, slouched on the sofa. He's relaxed in his worn t-shirt and old sweats. His hair is messy, and he looks exhausted, probably from all the overtime he's been working.

She swallows as she glides into the room. He doesn't notice her right away, and she worries she's being too bold, but she made her decision, and she's not one to back down.

Alec looks up from the TV with a slight gasp as he notices her. He sits up straighter, grabbing the remote to pause his show. He slides a hand through his hair attempting to arrange it. "Morgan, what are you doing here?"

A tiny grin curves her lips. She caught him off guard and made him nervous. It's uncharacteristic for him to show the anxiety he buries beneath his charm. She knows him better than anyone and knew him before he learned how to hide behind his charm and charisma. Not only that, he called her Morgan, not Fletch or Fletcher. She takes a step forward, enjoying his nervous tics. He's straightening out his clothes, rearranging his hair. He looks like he isn't sure if he should sit forward or stand or pretend to play it cool by staying where he is.

Morgan's grin grows. "I broke up with Preston," she says like it's new information.

He looks confused, so she continues, "I wanted to make sure you were aware."

Alec sits forward. "Oh, yeah?"

Morgan places a knee on the couch next to him. She kneels, facing him, and Alec holds his breath. "Yep, he wasn't the right person for me."

"No one is good enough for you, Morgan." Alec reaches for her, his palm caressing her cheek as his hazel eyes search hers before glancing at her lips. "Morgan, why are you here?"

She bites her lip, all her earlier courage gone. "You scare me, Alec, but I can't keep pretending that everything you do, doesn't affect me."

Alec sighs, closing his eyes for way too long, leaving Morgan no clue what he's thinking. She can't go through another round with him. Her heart won't survive it, and she didn't come here to back down. Morgan leans into him, her body pushing him deeper into the couch. She presses her lips against his unsuspecting mouth and realizes what she is doing is crazy. She moves to pull back, but his arms wrap around her, drawing her chest to his. He guides her lips, gently brushes his tongue against their crease.

With a quick inhale, her body melts into his as she straddles him. His tongue separates her lips, and she welcomes it like a lost friend coming home. Years of emotions are wrapped up in this kiss. Their lips, tongues, hands, and bodies move together in a desperate frenzy producing joyous relief from a decade of pent up desire.

CHAPTER 17

MORGAN LOWERS herself to the floor of the master bedroom because laying on the bed seems inappropriate. Actually, none of this seems right. She would lay in the living room, but it's covered in glass and debris from the brothers fighting.

Alec grabs a pillow from the bed and lays next to her. He pulls her into him, kissing her forehead the way he's done a thousand times. She wiggles up until their mouths align, and she kisses him, unsure what their future brings, but being smack dab in the middle of Jerrick's tragedy makes her hyper-aware of what she has to lose.

It took so long for her and Alec to become what they are, and she is terrified of losing what they have. "Alec, I don't want to lose you."

"I'm not going anywhere." He tucks a piece of hair behind her ear as they lay facing one another.

She bites her lip, trying to hold in all of her emotions.

"Morgan," he breathes, "I'm not gonna let anything happen to you."

"What about you?"

"Nothing's gonna happen to me. I'm not worried about that when I've got you on my team."

She presses her body against his, clinging to his back. "You always know what to say."

His lips brush her ear, and he exhales, "Because I know you." He kisses the side of her neck and pulls her closer.

"I know you too," she says. "I thought you were just the thorn in my side, but then you had to go and make me fall in love with you."

"Mmm, yeah, I did." He nibbles her neck and then pulls away from her, rolling onto his back. "We've gotta stop with the full-body contact."

She rolls on top of him, her legs straddling his hips while she leans down until her face is inches from his. "Or what?" she challenges.

He groans, "You can probably feel the or what pressed between your thighs."

She grins, moving her hips. "Are you trying to be modest on my account?"

"Hell yeah, I am."

"Why?"

"Because it's you, and you're the innocent one."

She pulls back. "I'm not all that virtuous. You make me sound like a nun."

"You're a fucking saint compared to me. I don't want to corrupt you."

Her forehead scrunches as her brows go up. "I'm sorry, what?

"My track record is—"

She holds up a hand to stop him. "Trust me, I know your track record, but how many of them did you love?"

He shakes his head.

"None of them, Alec. But you love me, and you loving me is not corrupting me."

"I just want to take it slow with you. I want to remember all of our firsts instead of rushing through them."

She laughs. "You sentimental sap." She leans down, saying, "I promise to take it slow, but I need you to kiss me."

THEY FALL ASLEEP WRAPPED TOGETHER, but before long, they wake to a noise outside the bedroom door. Morgan feels a tickle in her subconscious—the sensation Patrick taught her to recognize when an Olvasho is attempting to read her thoughts.

Quietly she whispers, "Three point one four one five nine two six five three five eight—" she motions for Alec to follow her as she crawls under the bed.

It's a tight fit, but he follows, and once they are lying flat, Alec breathes, "What the hell are you saying?"

"If I'm thinking of the numbers of pi, then they can't read my thoughts."

"You memorized pi?"

"I told you I memorized a lot of things. Count backward from one-thousand in threes," she whispers before going back to, "Three point one four one five—"

"You're such a nerd," he says with a dimpled grin. "Another thing I love about you." He kisses her temple. "Do you have to do it out loud? You know they're gonna find us."

"Not if Jerrick gets them first," she says.

Alec watches as she mouths each number, saying, "Do you think he came back?"

Morgan's numbers falter as she remembers how Jerrick left. "Of course," she breathes, "Maybe. I um, shh, we can't think about that. Three point . . . " Doubt creeps into her thoughts.

What if Jerrick had abandoned them? She tries to keep the numbers at the forefront of her mind, but she doesn't know how much good it's doing.

The door opens. Light floods the room. Morgan tries to even out her breathing, as her fingers intertwine with Alec's. She looks at him, his face so close to hers. He appears calm, even giving her a small smile like he used to give her when they were kids about to get in trouble. She envied his calm back then, but right now, she doesn't understand it. He shouldn't look so calm, unless they already had a hold on him.

The masculine voice comes from the doorway, demanding, "Get out here, now!"

It is the same voice from the lake—the voice that must belong to Keith.

She clings to the numbers like they can save her mind. Like she has a choice whether or not to listen to the compulsion that commands her to get out from under the bed. She fights it. Patrick had protected her mind to the best of his ability, but as her fingers unlace from Alec's, she knows it wasn't enough. She can't fight the impulse.

She climbs out, and Keith demands, "Stand up."

She does, looking over to see Alec standing on the opposite side of the bed. He's not looking at her. With a blank expression, he stares at Keith.

Two men enter the bedroom behind Keith. The first saying, "No sign of them. I don't know why the fuck Jerrick would come back here."

The other says, "He's sentimental."

"Looks like his emotions got the best of him once again," Keith says. "Let's get them in the car before he gets back."

Morgan watches and listens, her mind her own, while her will complies with Keith's commands. When he tells them to walk silently to the car, she and Alec walk in silence to the vehicle at the curb outside. They climb into the trunk, and when Keith says sleep, Morgan falls asleep.

ALEC WAKES with a throbbing head and a bloody lip. It takes him a moment to remember himself, and then he realizes he's no longer in Jerrick's house. He's sitting next to Morgan in an empty warehouse, tied loosely to a chair while the men who abducted them stand in a cluster a dozen feet away.

After Keith demanded they fall asleep, Morgan seemed to go under right away, but Alec didn't.

"Patrick made a mess of your mind," Keith had said. "Doesn't matter. You'll submit to me one way or another." Keith clubbed him in the head with something hard.

Alec looks at Morgan. She's awake, looking around the room. Her lips move slightly, and he knows she's still reciting pi. He taps her leg three times, the way they've always done, and her head snaps towards him.

"Do you know where we are?" Alec asks.

She shakes her head, whispering, "No."

The men turn their way, and one says, "So, she does have thoughts other than numbers."

Alec snorts, and Morgan nudges him.

"What?" Alec says, "It's funny. They tied us to chairs." Alec lifts his arms, loosening the unfastened ropes. "And not even well," he says through a laugh.

"I'm glad you find this so funny," Keith says.

"It's fucking adorable and completely pathetic. The girl beside me fought off Sky's son, giving him a bloody nose and holding a knife to his throat, before deciding she wouldn't kill him. Have you actually seen what Lathe can do? Have you seen what Emily, Patrick, and Jerrick are capable of?"

The men take a menacing step forward, and Alec continues, "Fucked, fucked, fucked. You are sooo fucked."

Keith holds his hand out to the others, so they stop while he continues forward. "I know what they can do, but look at you. Helpless. Hopeless. Hanging on to your insults because it's the only thing you have. Like you said, completely pathetic."

Morgan says, "Before you hurt us anymore than you already have, you should know, Emily is my best friend. What do you think she'll do to you if you hurt us?"

"Emily is cracked. It's only a matter of time until the Olvasho kill her. Besides, no one has seen my face, but you two."

"They know who you are, Keith," Alec says, "You've already been caught."

Instead of gasping as Alec thought, Keith shrugs. "It doesn't matter. Like I said, it's only a matter of time until they all kill each other."

"So, what's your goal?" Morgan asks.

Keith gives her a look. "What gives you the idea that I would tell you my plan?"

"You seem like the type that likes to talk about yourself," Alec says.

Morgan notes, "If you wanted to kill us, you would've done it already, so there has to be something you want from us."

Alec can feel Keith trying to search his mind, but Keith was right. His brain had been fucked with before, and for some reason, it seemed to make him more resistant to Olvasho tampering.

"Emily is not untouchable," Keith says, watching them, trying to see inside their minds.

Morgan interrupts with, "You want information on Emily."

Keith glares at her, and she begins to stand. "Sit down!" He commands, pointing at her.

She lowers back onto her seat. The ropes have mostly fallen away, leaving only Keith's will to hold them in place.

Alec laughs. "Who is this incompetent at tying ropes?"

"People who never work with their hands," Morgan replies.

Keith points at both of them. "We don't have to work with our hands. Not when we have the powers we have. We are the most powerful group in the world, and we are led by an unstable child. But not for long. She's already a mess. I only need to shove her over the edge."

Morgan can sense Keith trying to get in her head, but anytime he looks too closely, she begins with the numbers.

"Stop with the fucking numbers," he shouts, losing his cool.

He might be able to bend her will, but he has no power over her thoughts, and she watches him get angrier.

"Tell me Emily's weakness," he demands.

Morgan responds out loud, "Three point one five one—"

"SHUT THE FUCK UP!" he shouts.

She stops talking. She doesn't want to, but her physical responses are much more receptive to his commands.

Keith grins and pulls a chair over to sit face to face with Morgan. "You can't fight me."

She tries to calm herself, commanding her will not to comply with him.

Keith leans forward. "Tell me Emily's biggest weakness."

Morgan opens her mouth, the words on the tip of her tongue. "Three point—"

"Why are you not complying?!" he shouts, before turning to Alec. "Tell me her greatest weakness."

Alec says, "Trusting in people like you. Does she make you feel impotent?"

Keith backhands Alec and stands, kicking the chair he was using out of the way. He swings back to Alec and Morgan as he pulls a knife out of his pocket, snapping it open. "There is another way to do this," he says, inspecting the sharp blade. "It's how we got Jerrick's sister to comply."

Morgan's nostrils flare, and she tries to pull out of Keith's hold, but he reinforces his command. "Don't move."

She warns, "You will regret this."

Keith laughs. "Your group of misfit friends can't save you. They can barely handle themselves."

Alec says, "You killed Jerrick's sister?"

Keith grins. "Do you want to know what we did to her?"

Alec rolls his eyes. "Probably something that made you feel like a real man, but please tell me in your own words how intimidating and scary you are. It's totally working."

Morgan laughs, and Keith launches at her, gripping her neck with his free hand and pointing the knife at her face. Alec stops pretending to be mentally restrained and grabs the fist holding the knife. He jerks Keith's wrist behind his back as he loops the rope around Keith's neck. Then Alec grips the line and pulls, forcing Keith to let go of Morgan. He spins him around, putting Keith between himself and the two men that are coming at them.

"Stop," Alec demands, tightening the rope and pulling Keith back a step. "I'll kill him." He squeezes the noose, strangling him and twisting his arm until the knife falls from Keith's hand. Morgan picks it up.

The men step forward, and Morgan pokes Keith in the back with the tip of the blade.

Keith wheezes, "Stop."

The men hesitate, one saying, "You won't kill him."

The door behind the men slowly creaks open with a long ominous protest from the rusted hinges. Everyone freezes. And then a massive shadow fills the doorway. Jerrick's face hides beneath the shadow of his hood, reminding Alec of the grim reaper. A chill runs through him as Jerrick removes his hood and steps inside.

The men raise their hands in surrender.

Jerrick ignores them, walking right past them as if they don't exist. His deep baritone rumbles, "Alec, let go."

He releases the rope, and he and Morgan take a step back, their hands interlacing. Keith stands still, either by fear or because Jerrick is holding him in place. Jerrick stares at Keith as he moves forward. When he's standing directly in front of him, he says, "Morgan, Alec, the SUV is equipped with a holding cell in the very back. It's all set up if you would escort those two men out. They shouldn't give you any trouble."

"Okay," Morgan breathes, tugging on Alec's hand. They move toward the door, and Jerrick adds, "Best if you guys wait in the car too."

They walk outside into the drizzling rain. The SUV is close with the tailgate sitting open. The men climb inside the steel cell that sits behind the second row of seats. A solid barrier separates the two spaces.

As Alec closes the tailgate, he says, "I wondered what that wall was there for when we were in here earlier."

"Aren't you glad you didn't ask," she says.

He turns to her, taking her face in his hands and kissing her, letting out a breath of relief, and breathing her in. "You're my entire world, Morgan. I don't know what I'd do without you."

Her hands cover his. "Were you faking the whole time in there?"

"Most of it," he answers, "His commands didn't work on me. I had to bide my time until we were in the right position. That's why I kept trying to piss him off."

Morgan laughs. "And here I thought it was just your pleasant personality."

He kisses her again, but they're interrupted as the rain falls harder. Instead of getting in the car, they go back inside the warehouse to see what's going on.

They step inside, watching Keith and Jerrick from the doorway.

"What are they doing?" Alec whispers.

"Jerrick is probably interrogating him mentally."

"He's not gonna like what he finds," Alec comments.

They watch, waiting to see what fate Jerrick has for Keith.

JERRICK LOOKS deep into the recesses of Keith's mind.

Sky was like a God. He walked into the room, and everyone oohed and awed over him. Everyone wanted to impress him, including Keith, but Sky had rejected him one too many times. He no longer desired to be Sky's protégée. He wanted to destroy Sky for underestimating him, so he plotted against him, following Sky's every move, careful to stay in the shadows.

Keith heard rumors about a man with extraordinary gifts. If the rumors were true, Keith didn't want to be on the receiving end of those dangerous gifts, but he would love to direct them towards Sky.

They often held council meetings in different locations because Sky had moments of paranoia. With so many people wanting to kill him, his fear was well-founded. Thus, the next time Sky had a paranoid moment, Keith had the perfect venue for them, near the location of the rumored man. And to Keith's delight, the man himself showed up to the open meeting. There were four brothers, but only one of them had the gift rumored to be lethal. Keith didn't know which one, but they were all there, along with their beautiful sister.

Sky and Patrick left right after the meeting, leaving all of

Sky's goons behind. Most of them were simple-minded men, blindly following Sky because they loved violence and power. Laws didn't apply to them. They could quite literally get away with murder.

It was easy for Keith to manipulate them—pointing them toward the beautiful woman by warning them of how dangerous she was and how she knew secrets that could kill Sky.

Keith followed them that night, staying within earshot, and she didn't give them any information on what she knew. Eventually, Sky's goons got bored with her and left her for dead. Even half-dead, she made it all the way to her brother, Jerrick's house, but Keith couldn't let her live. She wasn't a stupid girl, and Keith couldn't chance this coming back on him, so he caught up to her halfway through the side yard and snapped her neck. He left her in the flower bed for her brother to find. And no one suspected a thing from Keith.

JERRICK STANDS in front of Keith, staring down at him, his eyes nothing but shadows. His clenched jaw and flexing fists give Morgan the impression he might tear Keith apart limb by limb, pulling his extremities off like plucking the legs from a spider.

"I am a God-fearing man," Jerrick growls. "I try to live peacefully, but I have murder on my soul, and one day, I will be judged. But when a snake sneaks into my home and kills my family, I will cut off its head and burn its body. I can't see your heart, but I see the truth inside your mind. I do not regret my choices. And you should know her name was Stacy and people miss her every day, whereas no one will miss you. No one will cry for you. No one will remember your name. I will cut off your head and throw you into the fire, and no one will even notice you're gone."

Jerrick takes a step back as blood trickles from Keith's eyes. Keith chokes and gags, sputtering up blood. It drips from his nose and streams from his ears, a pool gathering at his feet. With a final gurgling gasp, Keith collapses.

Jerrick looks down at the limp body for a second before turning to walk away. He doesn't seem surprised to see them watching from the doorway. He moves toward them, calmly as if he hadn't just killed a man. When he reaches Morgan, his palm cups her cheek, and he wipes away the tear that falls. He leans in to kiss her forehead, saying, "I'm sorry I left you, but I won't apologize for killing him." He steps back, acknowledging them both. "I'm sorry for the way I behaved before. It won't happen again. With that said, you guys did good. I'm impressed with both of you. And Alec, something is going on with you. Your mind feels distant. It's more than what Patrick did. I had a hard time sensing you at all. Your mind is like a flickering light."

"What the fuck does that mean?"

"I don't know, but I usually can sense people when they are near. They are like a glowing light in my mind. Even after Patrick protected Morgan's mind, her light hasn't dimmed though it is harder to get into her mind. But you, your light is like a flickering candle. Sometimes I can see it and sometimes I can't.

"Does that mean I'm dying or something?"

"I don't know what it means. I can't sense the Latovian people at all, but we would know by now if you were Latovian. Maybe you just have more control over it. Either way, now isn't the time to delve into this. We have prisoners to drop off, and I have to get you guys home."

CHAPTER 18

ELEVEN YEARS AGO ~

THE TEACHER STANDS at the front of the classroom and calls, "Alec, read the next paragraph."

His heart skips a beat, then hammers in his chest as he looks down at the book. The harder he concentrates, the more the words jump around on the page. He swallows as the temperature increases. Before the beads of sweat work their way down his neck, and his cheeks turn red, he straightens and clears his throat. He makes up his own words, improvising a more exciting story than the one he's supposed to read. A few of his classmates' chuckle and giggle and those noises make him continue until the teacher is right in front of him, shutting his book.

Alec leans back in his chair and continues his story even as the teacher glares at him. His classmates are all out laughing now. He looks up, and his friend Ben is shaking his head even as he laughs.

Ms. Grabill interrupts his comedy show by saying, "Alec Garner, Principal's office, now!"

He smiles, relieved he got through another day without them realizing he can't read. Granted, he had been held back in second grade, but somehow he had made it to fourth grade on his charm and memorization.

As he walks down the hall to the principal, he passes Morgan at her locker. They had been inseparable until he had to repeat the second grade. Now she was a big fifth-grader, and he was a dumb fourth-grader with a reputation. He tried to sneak past her, suddenly embarrassed by his behavior.

She notices him and turns around, smiling when she sees it's him. "Alec, did you get in trouble again?"

He shrugs with a smile. "I was just giving the people what they want. That reading is boring anyway."

"You got in trouble in reading again?"

"Ms. Grabill just doesn't like me."

She looks thoughtful a moment before saying, "Alec, you can read, can't you?"

He jerks back like he'd been struck. "Of course I can read. I'm not an idiot."

"No, but maybe you have a learning disability or something."

"I'm not disabled!"

"I mean like dyslexia or ADD. Do you have trouble paying attention or reading?"

"I'm fine, Fletch. Stop acting like a smartass fifth-grader!" Alec walks away.

Morgan runs after him, grabbing his arm. "I just hate seeing you in trouble all the time. I don't want you to end up in juvie."

"They aren't gonna send me to juvie for this stuff. You need to calm down."

She stands in front of him and grabs his hands, looking him

in the eye. "Alec, ask them to test you for dyslexia. If you don't, then I'll tell your mom, and she'll make you do it."

He pulls away. "You're so uptight. Why do you even care?"

"Because you're my friend, Alec. And you can't be mad at me for helping you."

"I don't need your help," he says.

"Yes, you do, and you should be used to it by now because I've always had your back, just like you've always been the thorn in my side. That's the way it's always gonna be."

ACKNOWLEDGMENTS

I have so many to thank, but much like this novella, I'm going to try to keep it short.

A huge thank you to my loyal readers! You guys rock! Thank you for following Emily's story.

I would not have completed any of the books I've written without the help of Mary Catherine Kline. This is the first thing I've written since she passed away, and it was so very bitter-sweet.

To my Mom and sisters, thank you for not only putting up with all my messages but also for being excited and encouraging. I love you all.

To all of my beta readers, your input is like gold. You make each book that much better, and I can't thank you enough.

Melissa Di Rienzo, you are incredible! After all you've gone through this year, you still carve out the time to help with my books. Thank you for all you have done. You truly are my unofficial assistant!

Justin, this novella wouldn't have happened without you. Thank you for loving this difficult, sensitive, stubborn woman.

SNEAK PEEK AT BOOK FOUR

BROKEN ALLIANCE PROLOGUE

SIX MONTHS AGO ~

Lathe lit up his phone, holding it out to see in front of him. He found his mother curled on the floor by the sofa in her modified basement apartment. She whimpered when the light illuminated her features.

"Mother, what do you see?"

"Gore," Evelyn whispered, uncurling from the fetal position to look at him with cloudy eyes. "Gore . . . and an army of horned beasts and fire. Fire burning everything." Her eyes grew wider as if what she was seeing was happening right in front of her. "Fire burning everything!" She folded back into a ball, covering her head with her arms. "No, no, no, no, no, no, no."

Lathe breathed out a sigh and put his phone away. He crouched to sit on the floor next to her, his back resting against the side of the sofa while he placed a reassuring hand on his mother's back, hoping she was only having a delusion and not a vision of the future, but he knew better. Delusions didn't incite such an emotional reaction from her. Lathe knew something bad was coming, but how could he possibly prepare when the details were so vague.

SNEAK PEAK AT BOOK FOUR

CHAPTER 1

Fire rains down from the heavens as winged demons fly through the night sky, exhaling flames. The mansion and stables burn while frightened horses run wild across the vast landscape. In the center of the chaos, riding fearlessly on the back of a snow-white horse is the scarred face of a warrior. Lathe shouts at the night sky, his face contorting with anger as he lashes out with violent winds.

Emily's blond hair flows out behind her, her beautiful face dusted with soot and streaked with tears as she comes from the woods riding on the back of a giant horned elk. Following her is a horde of horned beasts leaping out of the woods. She joins up with Lathe in the meadow just as a hippo sized dragon swoops down from the sky, breathing fire. Emily grabs the horns of her massive elk and rises to her feet on its back. She thrusts her arm out, shooting white-hot flames from her palm. There is no chance for the dragon to dodge the blaze, and as it strikes the beast, its cringe-worthy screams penetrate the air, sounding almost human. The creature spirals to the earth, breaking the ground and silencing its cries forever.

Hearing the call of their fallen brother, the dragons swarm, circling the meadow. Their sizes vary, from two-hundred pounds to two-thousand with bat-like wings that span from ten to twenty feet. Dozens of the hideous creatures come from all directions.

Lathe uses the air around him as a weapon, using sharp winds to throw his enemy off course, while Emily uses her gifts to leap onto the back of a deformed dragon flying too close. Her fingers grip onto the slimy skin of the beast, and before it throws her, she melds her mind with it.

Its stench is overwhelming, like a rotting corpse mixed with spoiled milk and mold. She forces the dragon up, flying higher into the sky. Her body slips down the creature as a chunk of the dragon's flesh sloughs off in her hand. She cringes, gagging as she drops the fleshy piece and grabs another area of the beast.

Once she's up high enough, she looks around, searching beyond the burned mansion and plumes of smoke covering the ground. Over the next hill, Emily spots what she's looking for and sends the dragon into a dive.

The mother dragon sits on the hillside looking regal. Its forty-foot wingspan dwarfs the others, and her flesh is covered in glistening purple and green scales making her body shimmer. The scales make the dragons flame-retardant, but none of the other dragons have them.

Emily dives through the sky, silent except for her heartbeat hammering. She realizes her dragon's stench is giving her away as the scaled beast sniffs the air and turns to face her. She swerves to the side, and her dragon loses its balance and spirals. Emily lets go and pads her fall, using the air to cushion her landing, while the deformed beast that was once human dies upon impact. These creatures weren't built to last. They were created to kill. Emily rolls up to her feet, and the ground rumbles as the mother dragon stalks towards her.

As it comes closer, Emily notices what she didn't before. On the back of the mother-dragon sits a Latovian warrior. Ashley turns her blond head, pinning Emily with her dark glare.

Emily shouts, "Ashley, don't do this!"

Ashley shakes her head, disgust curling her lips. "You've forced our hand!" She spits, "It's the only option you've left us!"

"Lathe is over there!" Emily warns, shouting to be heard. "Your dragons will kill him!"

Ashley's gaze flicks down for a moment before returning to Emily, her voice vibrating with rage, "Then let him die!"

Ashley yanks on the dragon's reins, and a thunderous rumbling begins inside the beast. Its neck stretches up, and its mouth opens, filling the heavens with the fires of hell. Then the creature turns her flames to engulf Emily.

Ashley cries out, her triumph tainted with grief.

The present comes back to Ashley as a cold sweat breaks out across her skin. It's always a little too chilly down here for her liking, but Latovia stayed a mild fifty to sixty degrees.

Hundreds of years ago, the Olvasho made it so the sun—the very source of Latovian magic—would kill Latovians should the sun or its shadow touch their skin, so now they are stuck here, underground in Latovia.

The glow of magic gemstones in the cave walls illuminates the room. They still glow gold, the color of Evelyn's magic. Evelyn was half Latovian, half Olvasho which is how she survived both sides of the portal, but even her immense power didn't stop a bullet from killing her.

Ashley doesn't have an ounce of Olvasho blood, but she has twice the amount of power a Latovian usually holds, which allows her to absorb the sun's energy. At least for now.

She sits on a hard seat with her back ramrod straight,

holding her composure. Her visions are coming more frequently, and each time they feel more alive than they did before. She tries to hide her trembling, remaining stoic as the needle repeatedly bites into her wrist.

Latovian tattoos are inscribed without the use of modern technology. Each stick of the needle burns like a swarm of bee stings, because mixed in the tattoo's ink, is Latovian magic.

First, a Latovian gemstone is melted down, the magic extracted and mixed with the ink. Then a custom-made needle, wielded by the precise hand of a carver, pierces the skin over and over again. The process is grueling, taking hours to complete two of the three thin bands around Ashley's wrist. She stays strong through the first two bands but feels faint by the end of the third.

"We'll finish in the morning," Wolfe announces in his gravelly voice. He speaks a little more stern, using the voice of authority—the voice of a king. People don't question him.

The carver is already packing up supplies. Ashley's shoulders stay ridged, her posture perfect as the surrounding group ready themselves to leave. Wolfe stands across from Ashley as everyone files out. His nearly black eyes meet hers, communicating understanding and compassion. His ebony skin and long dreadlocks almost match his black dragon skin jacket and pants. He looks like a shadow—one you wouldn't want to cross in a dark alley.

When Wolfe was sixteen, he killed the previous king, not in the traditional battle challenge, but by slicing the king's throat as he slept. What Wolfe did was ruthless, illegal, and punishable by death, but it didn't stop the Latovian people from demanding Wolfe take kingship. He was the only Latovian king voted into his role.

Wolfe closes the door after the last person exits the room. As soon as he flips the lock, Ashley's shoulders slump, her head falling back, while she lets go of her tears. Wolfe walks over to her, encouraging, "You did good today."

She lifts her head to glare at him, her inky eyes furious. "These traditions are barbaric!"

"It is the Latovian way."

"That doesn't mean it's right!"

"No, but traditions take time to break. You didn't cry. They will respect you more for your bravery."

Strands of blond hair fall in her face as she inspects the simple lines around her wrist. She expects her skin to be swollen and red, but her pale skin is flawless, marked only with the delicate black bands around her wrist.

She pushes her hair back, tucking it behind her ear as she looks up at Wolfe. "Can I go?"

"The tattoo is not complete, but I'm not holding you here."

She wipes her tears as she stands. "Where is Deja?"

"I told her to stay with him."

Deja is Lathe's favorite Latovian, aside from Ashley. The eight-year-old has more courage and gumption than any adult Ashley has met. Her spirit seems unbreakable, especially given the way her life began. When Deja was a toddler, her father challenged Wolfe in a fight to the death. When Deja's father lost, Deja's mother was ashamed and took Deja with her as she walked out into the sunlight. The sunlight killed Deja's mother instantly as the curse the Olvasho placed against those with Latovian blood burned through her body. Children were immune to the curse, so after Deja watched her mother die, she found shelter in the stables behind the Vallor mansion. Lathe was the one who found her and cared for her until Wolfe came to retrieve her during the new moon, the only time the Latovian curse is suspended. Lathe handed Deja over, but the two had already bonded, and their bond had only grown over the years.

Wolfe walks Ashley to the portal door. She has not yet

completely succumbed to her Latovian blood, but things are getting worse, and she knows it is only a matter of time until she can no longer leave Latovia.

Before she walks out of the portal, Wolfe reminds her, "Set your timer. Remember to watch your tattoos."

She nods. "See you soon," she says, holding back the tears that always threaten.

Lathe and Deja are right outside the portal, waiting on her. The once dank unwelcoming tunnel below the mansion was becoming a livable space thanks to all of Lathe's hard work. The biggest problem is its massive size. The arched stone ceiling above them is easily thirty feet high, and the tunnel itself is the size of a football field. Yet, Lathe works tirelessly on the space to make it more comfortable for Ashley.

Deja runs to Ashley. Her jet-black hair and eyes nearly as dark are stark in contrast to her pale skin. She is tiny for an eight-year-old, but her size only makes her more fierce.

Ashley thinks she's going to get a hug, but Deja pushes Ashley's sleeve up to view the new black bands around her wrist. "So cool! I can't wait to get my own," she says, looking at her own wrists.

Ashley barely holds back her wince. The day she gets her tattoo will be the day she can't come visit Lathe anymore, and she's afraid that will hurt him even more than her own absence.

"You still have some time, Deja. Enjoy your freedom while you have it," Ashley reminds her.

Deja wraps her little arms around Ashley in a quick hug, before leaving through the portal door.

Ashley looks up to find Lathe staring at her from ten feet away. Others may call him intimidating or sinister because of the horrific scars along the left side of his face and torso, but all Ashley sees is the beautiful man she fell in love with. Without his scars, she fears he would be too pretty. She loves every rough part of him, and the scars speak volumes about what kind of man he is. He was a teenager when he deformed himself in order to save his mother. It was one of many sacrifices. He has spent his whole life protecting those who can't defend themselves.

Seeing him now, Ashley is reminded of the vision she had earlier, the vision of him riding horseback across a burning lawn with dragons flying above.

Her visions began shortly after Evelyn died. She didn't think much of them at first, just vivid daydreams, completely inconsequential, but then her little daydreams started coming to life. They were small, little snippets of reality before they happened. Now her visions have grown elaborate and ominous.

Lathe's eyes don't miss a thing as he steps forward. "You had the vision again?"

She nods, her eyes blurring.

He pulls her against his chest, and she takes in his scent as her finger claw into his back, holding onto him as if it will hold off the inevitable.

Visions of the future were Evelyn's thing, but when Evelyn killed Ashley, she merged their souls to save Ashley's life. Now, Ashley sees pieces of the future.

"What are we gonna do, Lathe?"

SNEAK PEEK AT BOOK FOUR

CHAPTER 2

Ominous clouds blanketed the May sky, threatening showers. The ground, over-saturated from a week's worth of rain, squishes beneath Patrick's boots as he walks through the lush green lawn from the Fort Wayne mansion to the stables around back. The pasture is rife with spring noises. Crickets chirp, birds sing, and insects buzz by as Patrick tromps through the high grass. If he had realized sooner how tall the grass was, he would have taken the driveway back. He swats at a bug before pulling his hood up over his short blond waves as it begins to rain.

He looks ahead, spotting Lathe outside on the far side of the barn. Lathe's boots nearly get stuck in the mud as he leads his snow-white horse toward the barn. Deja, perched on the back of the mare, notices Patrick. She points, and Lathe turns to look. Lathe switches direction, moving toward Patrick.

They meet just outside of the barn, but before Patrick speaks, the rain stops and wind stills. The chirping birds grow silent, and the crickets stop their song. The fine hairs on the back of his neck rise, and he looks across the lush pasture to the mansion, noting, "Emily's awake."

Deja asks, "How do you know?"

"The wind stopped," Lathe says.

"Don't you feel the stillness? The silence?" Patrick asks.

Deja takes in her surroundings and shivers. "That's creepy."

"How's she doing?" Lathe asks.

"Worse," Patrick answers without elaborating.

ALSO BY ANNA REZES

Continue Emily's story in *Broken Alliance*, the fourth book in the Valla Series.

VALLA SERIES:

Unraveling Emily ~ book one

Descendant of Valla ~ book two

Guardian of Latovia ~ book three

Broken Alliance ~ book four

Pink f*cking Moscato

ABOUT THE AUTHOR

Anna Rezes has been passionate about writing since she was a child. When she's not busy honing her superpowers or traveling to other worlds full of fictional characters, she is spending time with family and friends. She lives in Central Ohio with her husband, their two dogs, and the cat they love and hate. Anna is the author of *Unraveling Emily, Descendant of Valla, Guardian of Latovia, Broken Alliance,* and *Pink f*cking Moscato.*

For more from Anna Rezes visit:
www.annarezes.com
www.instagram.com/anna_rezes
www.facebook.com/annarezesauthor
www.twitter.com/annarezes

www.ingramcontent.com/pod-product-compliance
Lightning Source LLC
Chambersburg PA
CBHW020546130626
46552CB00007B/2778